T0114196

COULD HAVE BEEN A COWBOY

_____

Dedicated in memory of my friends Teresa Carr and Willie Masingale

COULD HAVE BEEN A COWBOY

By: Karen Fisher

Illustrated By: Willie Masingale

The sun shone down on Tonnie's face as she laid in the cool, tall, new, green grass. It was the best feeling in the whole world. If her Pa knew she was being a slackard on her chores he would surely take a strap to her.

The only thing that probably saved her was William, her big brother. He had done more than his share this morning. Pa was pleased with what he saw, when he came to the barn.

She opened her lazy eyes as she heard Pa calling her name. She jumped to her feet, and ran to the back of the barn. She walked around to the front of it, to be greeted by him. "Come on girl, what is wrong with you? If you want to go into town with William, and I you better get a move on!" It was a real treat to get to go with Papa to town. They hardly ever went with him.

Tonnie began to help William hitch up the team to the wagon. The excitement was building up inside of her. She past by William and whispered a thank you for saving her hide. He smiled because he knew he had surely done that. They climbed up in the wagon beside their Pa. Tonnie looked up at him. "Ma isn't coming with us? She asked him.

Pa said, "Your mother is feeling poorly lately. That is why I appreciate you two helping out so much. Lord knows she can use the rest."

Chapter 2

Pa stopped in front of the General Store. They climbed out of the wagon and went inside. Pa greeted the clerk Mr. Silvey. He began to tell him the supplies that he needed. As Mr. Silvey got the supplies, Tonnie and William carried them out to their wagon. By the time Pa finished they had it all loaded and ready to go. Tonnie and William waited for their Pa in the wagon. He was saying his good byes to Mr. Silvey.

A rowdy cowboy rode by screaming and he fired his gun into the air. It spooked the horses. William grabbed the reins. Tonnie screamed and grabbed hold of William who was trying to hold the horses.

Their horse Pacer, who is spooky anyway, reared in the air just as Pa tried to calm him. Pacer's hoof hit Pa right across the face and he went to the ground. Tonnie was screaming for her Pa and was climbing out of the wagon. Mr.

Silvey grabbed her and held her back. He told someone to go get the Doctor.

Pacer wouldn't have hurt Pa for the world. The cowboy had spooked him. A crowd gathered around Pa and Tonnie was trying to get free from Mr. Silvey's hold. "Please, let me go. I have to see about my Pa!" Men gathered around to help. They picked up Pa and carried him away.

William put his arms around Tonnie as she sobbed. He had feared the worst. He hoped Tonnie hadn't realized what just happened. Their horse Pacer....... had killed their Pa.

Chapter 3

Ma took the news hard and feeling poorly didn't help. She spent the next few months in bed and wouldn't eat. William was eight, and Tonnie was six years of age when their ma passed. The sheriff made all the arrangements and their Ma was placed beside their Pa. He then contacted the only relative he knew about. He sent word to their Aunt Effie he was putting them on the next stage out east to her. They had heard of their Aunt Effie, but they had never met her.

Tonnie didn't know if she liked that ideal. They didn't even know her. She didn't think it was fair to make them go when she didn't want to. William held her hand and was always comforting her. He would be there for her no matter what happened to them.

When the stage arrived out east their Aunt was waiting. It was as bad as Tonnie had feared it would be. Aunt Effie was older than their ma had been. She was mean and acted like she had been put upon. From the very time they arrived Tonnie felt that her and William weren't wanted.

Their Aunt Effie was well off, and she lived in a fine house and wore fine clothes. She bought all new clothes for them. She made them scrub in a tub for what seemed forever. It was like she couldn't get them clean enough. She burned most of the clothes they had brought with them.

How horrid she was. How would they ever be able to stay here? After everyone had gone to sleep Tonnie snuck down the hall to William's room. She climbed into bed with him and snuggled up to him. She sobbed. "William, I don't like it here. I don't want to stay here. I want to go home."

William said, "This is our home now Tonnie. We will have to make the best of it."

Aunt Effie didn't get along with Tonnie. Every little thing she did Aunt Effie would whip her. William would put his arms around her and let her cry. "Tonnie, why do you do those things to upset her?"

"Anything I do upsets her, William. I don't think she even wants me to breathe. She didn't like me right from the beginning. I don' t like her either!"

William said, "We have to make the best of things Tonnie, until we are old enough to take care of ourselves. When that day comes, everything will get better." He looked at her. "I promise! It has to get better!"

Chapter 4

We put up with all Aunt Effie had to dish out for eight long years. It was when she tried to decide William's life for him that he drew the line. During their argument she shouted, "As long as you are in this house you will abide by my rules."

He shouted, "I have tried to do that up until now, but you are not going to tell me who I can court. That is my decision alone. I am sorry Aunt Effie. I appreciate all that you have done for Tonnie and me, but I will not marry that woman just to please you! So I will be leaving here."

She thought him ungrateful and slapped him across the face. "You ungrateful little worm." Being the gentleman he was he stood there frozen in the moment as not to let his temper flare. He turned and walked out of the room and ran up the stairs to his room.

Tonnie ran up the stairs after him. He was already packing to leave. Tonnie said, "I'm going with you William."

"No!" He shouted at her. "You will stay here until I figure out what I am going to do. When I save enough money I will send for you."

"William, you can't be serious. You can't just leave me here!" Tonnie began to cry. "I don't know how I will make it without you William. Please say I can go with you!"

He wouldn't give in to her no matter how bad she cried. He just couldn't subject them both to not knowing what to do. He picked up his belongings, went down the stairs, and out the door. All Tonnie could do is cry and scream out his name. "Please don't leave me here!!!"

It had been two years since the day that Tonnie last saw William. He hadn't let her know what happened to him. He had never sent for her like he promised. Tonnie didn't even know if he was still alive. She had given up hope of seeing or hearing from him again.

Chapter 5

Although the sun would be setting soon, there was still life stirring. People were rushing around trying to get home before the weather set in. Tonnie was walking briskly home when the doctor spotted her. "Tonnie, what are you doing on the streets so late? Besides that you are going to catch your death of a cold in this dampness. Have you lost your mind? Come into the Hotel and let me buy you a cup of hot tea. At least it will warm you."

He was a friendly older gentleman and she wasn't scared to be with him. A shiver ran down her spine at his suggestion of it being so cold. She smiled at him as he held the door for her. They sat at a table and he ordered their drinks.

She unbuttoned her cloak, and pushed it off her shoulders to the chair she was sitting on. He said, "What are you doing out so late on a day like this?"

She said, "I have been in town all evening and I lost track of time. I really shouldn't be here. Aunt Effie will be so upset with me if she finds out I am not home. It is just I am chilled, and I appreciate the warmness of the tea. It is very kind of you."

He watched her as she sipped on the hot liquid. He said, "Have you heard the latest news?"

She shook her head to let him know she hadn't as she sipped her tea.

"A big plantation owner is in town. He is organizing a round up. The foreman will be signing on hands tomorrow in front of the Old South Meeting house. It will mean much needed work for most of the men. They will be taking the finest string of horses that I have ever seen to Richmond, Virginia. It is the most exciting thing to happen around here in a long time."

She pulled her cloak around her once again. She said, "I really must be going. I thank you once again for your kindness." She stood to leave.

The doctor walked her to the door. "Tonnie, you must promise me that you will go straight home. There are a lot of extra men in town, and the streets may not be safe for you."

"Yes sir, I am going straight home. Thank you, doctor."

He watched her walk away, as she hurried down the street. Once on the bridge she stopped walking. The view was breath taking. The sun was setting and left a reddish orange, and purple hue on the water. The water was rapidly swirling in turmoil as it went beneath the bridge. It reminded her of her emotions.

It was getting colder as she pulled the hood of her cloak more around her face. She could see her breath from the cold.

She stood motionless staring into the water. What was she going to do? No one knew how cruel her aunt was. It was almost unbearable to stay with her. She wanted to control Tonnie's life also and it was beginning to get horrid. She didn't beat her anymore, but Tonnie always tried to please her in every way possible. How could her brother have left without taking her with him? She was so angry with him for that.

She was standing there lost in her thoughts when some one grabbed her. Tonnie was too scared to scream. She began to struggle trying to free herself. "Unhand me this instance!"

The man said, "What, and let you jump into the cold water?"

What had he said? She had no intentions of jumping from the bridge into the frigid water. Not only was she at her wits end, but also she must have looked it too.

Once she made it clear to him that she wasn't going to jump he released his hold on her.

Her lips quivered. Mostly from being scared to death, but she was also trembling from the cold.

He said, "You are freezing. You must come with me to the Hotel. What you need is something hot to drink, you know, to take the chill off."

She tried to protest, but he wouldn't hear of it. So once again, she was taken to the Hotel for a second cup of hot tea.

He sat holding his hands around the hot cup of coffee. She was taking a better look at him. He was a very handsome, young man. He had dark curly hair, tanned skin, and the bluest eyes she had ever seen. Even though he seemed young it had her puzzled to the fact that he was acting much older than his years.

He glanced at her, and she was embarrassed that she was caught looking at him. He noticed her dancing green eyes and was smiling at her. Perhaps because he had to repeat what he said.

"Let me introduce myself so we won't be such strangers. My name is Robert James Devain, and who might you be?"

"My name is Tonnie Lisa Barrett."

He looked at her. "What a strange name!"

Tonnie laughed. "As the story goes.... when I was wrapped in a blanket and they first handed me to my papa the day I was born he said, "This baby weighs a ton." Thus being, my mama named me Tonnie."

He said, "I know that name, Barrett. Are you any kin to Lon Barrett?"

She hung her head. "I was his daughter."

"Was?" He said.

"Yes, he was killed in an accident when William and I were small. My mother died about a year after that. William and I were sent here to live with my aunt."

He said, "I am sorry to hear that. He was a good man."

She stood to leave and pulled her cloak around her once again. "I really must be going. I will be in big trouble as it is. I thank you for the tea." She turned to walk away.

Robert stood up and yelled, "Whoa! I will walk you home."

"That won't be necessary. I can make it home on my own."

"Nonsense!" He shouted as he walked with her out the door. She hurried her step to try to get home before her aunt noticed she was missing. After this second episode she would surely be caught.

She stopped in front of her house. Robert said, "Maybe we will see each other again. I will be here a couple of days."

She smiled at him and said, "Maybe we will, and I thank you again for the tea." She opened the door and slipped inside.

Chapter 6

Tonnie was smiling as she shut the door. She was going to try to slip upstairs before her aunt spotted her. "Lisa! Lisa Barrett, is that you?"

"Yes, auntie, it is I."

" Where have you been? Oh! Look at your clothes. You have ruined them in this weather. Don't you have any sense at all? I want you to go upstairs and change. Don't be slow about it." Her aunt said as she flipped her hand in the air. "Then I want you down here! Benton is in the parlor waiting for you. Hurry child, don't take all night."

For some time her aunt had been trying to get something started between Lisa and Benton. Lisa couldn't stand him.

He was sissy and could barely feel comfortable around a woman. She hurried up the stairs to escape.

She changed into dry clothes and sat there on her bed. All of the sudden her aunt began to squawk. "Lisa! Lisa, get down here." She didn't want to go, but she didn't want her aunt coming upstairs after her either.

When she entered the room Benton stood up. He stammered, "Hello, Lisa. Nice weather we are having!"

Tonnie stopped walking and glared at him. "Benton, it is horrid out there! There is nothing nice about it."

He was embarrassed that he said what he had. Her aunt said, "Lisa, don't be so rude to our guest. I will get right to the point. Benton has asked me for your hand, and I have accepted!"

Tonnie just stood there not believing what she heard. "You have what? I won't marry this man. I don't love him! You can't make me marry him! I won't! Do you hear me?"

Tonnie turned and rushed out of the room. Her aunt was yelling for her to come back, but she didn't care. She hurried up the stairs, trying not to cry and slammed her bedroom door. She was so furious that she couldn't keep from crying. This was exactly why William left. She had tried to plan his life for him also.

Rosa the servant tapped on the door. "Tonnie.... honey May I come in." Tonnie got up from the bed and opened the door.

"Oh, Rosa. What am I going to do? I won't marry that sissy man! I am going to have to leave."
Rosa reached into her apron. "Tonnie girl, this letter came for you today. It looks real important. I done an snuck it out of the mail before Miss Effie seen it."

Through Tonnie's tears she looked at the letter. "It is from William! He finally wrote to me. He is finally letting me know where he went." She ripped it open and began to read. He told her how sorry he was for taking so long to write. Then he told her he had bought a small farm in Richmond, Virginia. He was saving money and could probably send for her in a few months as he promised.
"Richmond Virginia?" That was the second time today that she had heard of that place.

Of course, it was the round up with all the horses. "Rosa, I am leaving here." She picked up the razor from her vanity. " I want you to cut my hair!"

"What? I can't do something like that. Your aunt will take a whip to me."

Tonnie said, "She won't ever know. Before she has time to see me, I will be gone from here. Oh Rosa, Please help me."

Rosa's hand was shaking as she began to cut Tonnie's long, beautiful curls. It wasn't long until her beautiful curls were falling to the floor at their feet. When Rosa was through cutting her hair, Tonnie went to William's room and found some of his clothes he had left behind. There were blue jeans, boots, a shirt, a leather vest, and a cowboy hat. She couldn't believe it. Everything fit her, that must have been why he left them. She found the six shooters her Pa had taught them to shoot with. It completed the outfit. Once she was dressed she looked into the mirror. It seemed as if a half grown, gun slinging.... boy was in the reflection. It was just the look that she wanted. She would have to pose as a boy to pull this off.

She gave Rosa a hug. Tears were streaming down her face because she knew Tonnie was leaving. Tonnie said, "Don't worry about me Rosa. I am going to be with William. I can't stay here another minute. I have to leave before auntie makes me marry that awful man. Goodbye Rosa!" She gave her another hug. Rosa was wiping tears with her apron as Tonnie slipped quietly out the door.

Chapter 7

That night Tonnie slept in the loft at the stable next to
the Ole South Meeting House. The next morning she planned
to sign up for the drive. She didn't know if she could get away
with it, but she had to find a way to be with William.

In the early morning she was awakened by the sounds of
men trying to break a black stallion. Men were flying off of
him, as fast as they were climbing on. He was a tough one all
right. She watched them for a while, and then she went to
sign on for the drive.
She nervously stood in line. She had to remember that she
was supposed to be a boy. Nobody could find out her secret.
She looked the part, now she would have to act it.

One of the men had to be helped off the ground after being thrown by the horse. The foreman that was signing on hands yelled, "Leave the black alone! If we can't brake him, he will just have to run with the others." After he said that he turned and looked at Tonnie. "Well, son what do you want?"

She cleared her throat and said, "I want to sign on for the drive." Everyone started to laugh.

The foreman said, "I don't think I can use you. Come back in a few years after you grow up!" Everyone began to laugh again.

She looked at him and said, "I can ride, and shoot as well as the rest of them. I know all there is to know about driving cattle, horses shouldn't be much different." (Of course all she knew about a cow was that it has two ears, four legs, and a tail, but he didn't have to know that.) " I want to sign on!"

One of the hands that had been laughing the most said, "Well boss, why don't you let this little guy prove himself. If he can cut it, sign him on."

The foreman said, "And just what do you suggest he do to prove himself?"

The hand said, "Let him brake the black."

The foreman said, "No! That black almost killed Sam. You can't expect me to let this boy try to ride him."

Tonnie said, "I'll ride him, and I'll brake him too! If I do, I'm going on the drive." She walked over and stepped through the rails of the corral before the foreman could stop her. Some of the hands were holding on to the black. Tonnie began to whistle a little tune. The black began to twitch his ears and listen to her. Everyone stood there laughing and making fun of her, but they didn't know she knew what she was doing. She began to rub his face, and nose, while whistling. The black liked to hear her whistle. When she would stop he would nudge her with his nose. She would rub his nose and start whistling again. He loved it just like she knew he would. She stepped away with her back to him. He would nudge her with his nose, and she would start to whistle the same tune.

She spent the next hour petting the black and whistling. The men thought this was the dumbest thing that they had ever seen. She stepped up into the saddle before they, or the

black thought about it. Her lightweight made it feel like she wasn't even there.

The horse acted stunned at first but then began to run, and buck about. However it wasn't as severe as he had done before. It wasn't long before she had him walking around the corral, and doing whatever she wanted him to.

One of the hands took off his hat, shook his head, and slapped his hat on his leg. He couldn't believe what he just witnessed. A boy broke the black. He opened the corral gate, and Tonnie rode up to the foreman.

He said, "Kid, you just earned a spot on the drive. You can have the gear and the Black for breaking him."

About that time a man walked up to the foreman. "Have we got enough men for the drive, Sidney?"

Sidney said, "Yes Boss, I think we do. Oh! By the way I gave the black and the gear to this kid. It was the craziest thing that I ever did see. A boy broke the black! I also gave him a job. He is young, but from what I saw, I think he can handle the job."

The boss said, "Well, we will see if he can. Once we leave he will have to handle it."

Tonnie took her things, and rode the Black into the stable as fast as she could. She almost choked when she saw the boss. What was she going to do now?

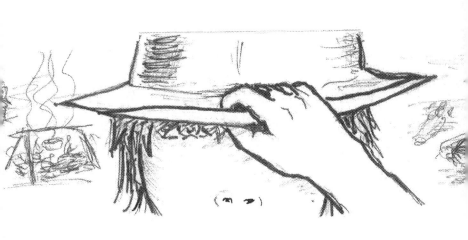

Chapter 8

That evening the boss rode up beside Tonnie. They had started the drive right after Sidney had signed on the last of the men. It was starting to get dusky dark. She had been stuck at the back of the Bermuda in all the dust and smell. She didn't protest. She had passed the test. At least she was getting to come along. That was the easy part. The hard part would be pulling it off.

When the boss rode up to her, she pulled her hat down a little trying not to be recognized.

"Howdy!" he said. "You must be the one that I have been hearing about. I am the boss of this outfit. My name is Robert J. Devain. And who might you be?"

Tonnie said, "Everyone just calls me kid. You can do the same." She kicked the black, and went riding after a couple of stragglers. After finding out that the boss was Robert she tried to avoid him as much as possible, for fear he would figure out who she was.

After they stopped the drive for the night some of the men sat by the campfire talking. Some had already bed down. Tom was playing his guitar and quietly singing. Tonnie made her bedroll away from the fire. She didn't want to be so noticeable, but not to far away because of the warmth and wild animals. No one had observed she was a girl, and she wanted to keep it that way.

The boss sat down on the log beside where she was bedding down. "Well kid, how did it go today?"

She said, "It wasn't so bad. I sort of liked it."

He said, "Good, I am glad you are getting along okay. You know kid; some of the men are talking about how strange you act. How you stay to yourself, and about the fact that you don't seem to want anyone to know much about you. You aren't running from any trouble are you?"

She looked at him. "No sir, I am not running from any trouble."

He said, "If you were you would come clean with me, wouldn't you?'

Tonnie said, "Yes sir, I would tell you if I was in trouble."

He slapped his legs and stood up. "That is good enough for me. Get some sleep kid. We are going to have a long, hard day tomorrow. Good night."

"Good night, Boss."

Tonnie got into her bedroll. She was aching from all the riding they had done. The fire was burning low, and she was almost asleep. She heard someone leaving the camp. She put on her boots to follow them. She didn't know who it could be. She probably wouldn't have followed them, but they were acting so sneaky about leaving. It didn't matter much anyway, because who ever it was, lost her. She finally went back to camp. She was tired, and it didn't take her long to fall asleep.

Chapter 9

The dawn was breaking into a new day. Most of the men were up stirring around. Claude noticed Tonnie still sleeping in her bedroll. He looked around, and then he threw his wash water on her. She tore out of her bedroll and the fight was on. "Why you dirty ole hound dog. I'll show you who to throw your dirty ole wash water on!" She put up a pretty good fight for her size, and she was just about more than Claude could handle. To top it off she was holding her own and fighting like a boy!

Everyone was laughing at his plight until the Boss came charging in to stop it all. He had taken hold of the back of Tonnie's clothes trying to hold her back. "What is this all about? Kid! Go get washed up for breakfast." He kind of tossed her around in the other direction. "Go on, get going!"

"I'll show that ole pole cat who to throw his wash water on!" She started for him again, and Robert grabbed her vest. He said, "Go do as I said." Tonnie went over and poured some water in the pan to wash up. She was so angry. Robert looked at Claude. "Get on your horse, get to work, and leave the kid alone! I'll have no more trouble." Robert left the camp.

Claude looked at Tonnie. "Don't forget to wash behind your ears sonny!" He began to chuckle at her as he stepped on his horse and rode off to start the day. Tonnie just glared at him. He was one she didn't have good feelings about. She had washed up and strapped on her six-shooters. She wouldn't think of starting the day without them.

She got a plate of food from Cookie and sat down on the log to eat. She was so mad at Claude that she choked on the coffee. Either that, or it was just too awful. What is this colored water she was drinking? All of the sudden something landed in her plate. She looked up, and Fred was sitting on his horse. His leg was folded in front of his saddle horn. He had spit tobacco in her plate.

She sat there a second, dropped her plate, and yelled, "All right mister! You just better get over there and get me another plate of grub."

He just sat there on his horse laughing at her. She pulled her gun and shot his hat off before anyone could blink. "I said, Move!"

He was a bit startled at first, and then he was furious. He was climbing down off of his horse. "Why you little snot nose. What you need is a good tanning. I'm going to tan your backside with the feel of leather." He was unbuckling his belt to take it off as he was coming toward her.

It hadn't scared her at all. "The next one will be right between those pole cat eyes mister!" He still rushed toward her. She hadn't ever shot anyone before, but she was trying to get her bluff in. "It looks as if you want an early grave mister."

In one quick move he had taken her gun away and threw her over his knee. He began to hit her with his belt. "Well, sonny we'll see how you like this?" He was hurting her, but she couldn't blubber and cry like a girl. She had to be tough. After all she was supposed to be a boy!

Robert rode up, and was climbing down off his horse before it had come to a complete stop. He had heard the gun shot. "What is going on here?" He stopped Fred from whipping her. She was standing there spilling out a mouthful of obscenities. Robert said, "What do you think you are doing? If there is any trouble you are to come to me!"

Fred said, "This sassy kid shot my hat off, and threatened to put the next one between my eyes. I was just showing him how I feel about that."

Robert looked at Tonnie. "Is that right, son?"

She said, "Yes sir, that is sort of right. He spit tobacco in my food and wouldn't get me more. I did shoot at him, but I was only trying to let him know he wasn't going to push me around."

He looked at Fred. "Is that right, Fred?"

"Yes, I recon it is."

"I want all of you that expect to have a job here to get to work! I don't want any more trouble out of any of you! Half the day is gone! Get to work!" Everyone began to scramble to their horses and some rode off for fear of losing their job.

Tonnie picked up her gun. Robert picked up her hat and handed it to her. He said, "Well kid, this is twice this morning that I have had to bail you out of trouble. I don't want you taking any more pot shots at the men."

She looked at him. "If you think that I am going to stand here, and let them run over me you've got another thing coming!" She began to mumble obscenities again.

He pointed his finger at her and said, " I won't have anymore such talk out of a youngster such as you! Next time I hear it, you may just find yourself across my knee."

Tonnie put on her hat. She was taking time to saddle the black while Robert was lecturing her. She stepped up on her mount to start work. By the fire in her dancing green eyes you couldn't help but know she was angry.

Robert began to laugh at her. She whirled the black around to face him. "What is so all fired funny?"

Robert said, "Hey, you better watch out kid. No matter what you think I am on your side."

Tonnie turned to face the other direction and raced away.

Chapter 10

Tonnie and the black began a day's work. By noon she was beginning to get the growls. "Dang polecat!" Robert was keeping an eye on her. For some unknown reason he liked the kid. He began to laugh when he saw her rub her belly. He rode up next to her. "How about a little beef jerky? It sure does help a man out between meals."

She reached out to take the beef jerky from him. "Thanks."

He said, "I'm sorry about this morning. It is just that I don't like hearing language like that from younger fella's such as yourself. It just doesn't seem right somehow. I also don't want you taking shots at the men. It is for your safety as well as for the others." He was smiling at her. He was looking so close at her she began to feel uncomfortable. She pulled her hat down a little more said, "Whatever, you say boss." She kicked the Black and rode away. He just watched her ride off in a wondering way. She hoped he would never figure out her secret. What will she ever do if he does figure it out? She was going to have to watch herself very carefully around him to make sure that didn't happen.

Chapter 11

By evening, she was worn out and ready to stop when they finally bed down for the night. The little red headed boy that helped the cook on the wagon was gathering firewood. Since Cookie had him so busy he asked Tonnie to go down to the river to retrieve some water.

She was stooped over getting the first bucket of water when Robert walked up. It seemed that she couldn't get shed of him. Every time she turned around he was there.

"Well, it looks as if Cookie has drafted you into a little extra duty." He was standing behind her and was so quiet that she didn't know if he was still there. He said, "You know kid, every once in a while I get the strangest feeling that I have met you somewhere before. Yes sir, I have racked my brain, but I just can't figure it out!"

Tonnie stood there frozen. He handed her the other bucket so she could fill it, but before she had hold of it he dropped it on the ground. He grabbed her by her shoulders. "Tonnie Lisa Barrett!!!" He was just about hysterical.

She said, "Shut up! Do you want somebody to hear you? I don't want anyone to know that I am a girl and you are about to spoil it!"

He was babbling on. "I have to send you back!"

She said, "The name is Tonnie, and I am not going back!'

He said, "Well, I have to see to it that you go back."

Tonnie said, "All right Bobby! Send me back, but you can't make me stay there. I will only leave again. You know I will!"

He said, "What about your aunt? Don't you think she is worried sick about you? But no, you wouldn't think about anything like that! What about William? Don't you think he would be worried?"

"William is why I am here! He left a long time ago, because our aunt wanted to tell him how to live his life. Where he could go, whom he could see. I didn't even know where he was until I got his letter the night we had tea. He is in Richmond. He has bought us a farm and was going to send for me. I couldn't wait that long. I had to go find him now! That is why I have to go there. This is the only way that I knew to get there."

"Tonnie, a trail is no place for. ...... A woman!"

"No one knows that I am a woman, and I intend to keep it that way! Hasn't it worked out so far?"

"Yes, but that was before I knew. I can't believe I didn't catch on. I should have known by your dancing green eyes. That is what finally gave you away."

She said, " I have pulled my weight so far Robert, and I won't go back!"

He said, "Don't you stand there and tell me what you will and won't do! I'll be the one to decide that!"

She said, "You are just my boss! You don't own me! I will do as I please!" Her eyes were dancing again. Cookie began to yell for the water. She grabbed the other bucket, filled it with water, pushed Robert aside, and went up the hill to the wagon with the water. Robert let out all his air and ran his hand through his black hair. He put on his hat, and walked up the hill after her. He felt he had his hands full now.

He just couldn't believe it took him so long to figure it out.

Chapter 12

After Robert found out Tonnie's secret, he stayed close by watching her every move. Some how she always found herself at the back of the Bermuda. Robert was watching her out of her view, when she rode upon a rattlesnake. It's warning spooked the black. He reared up. Tonnie did a summersault from the back of the horse and landed on her backside in the dust that flew up around her. The fall took her aback for a split second almost knocking the air from her. Nothing seemed to be broken. That is when she saw the snake getting ready to strike her. Robert was already off his mount and running toward her to see if she was all right. Like lightning

she drew her gun and shot the snake as he was in the air coming toward her. In one shot she had taken his head off. Robert had stopped running and was standing there with his mouth open. He couldn't believe what she did. She was an excellent shot just as she had stated before. Tonnie was so relieved that the snake hadn't bitten her. She fell back in the dust, and the dust clouds rose around her. Robert ran to her. "Are you all right, Tonnie?"

She said, "Well, I am not busted up, and I am not snake bit. That is a good thing. But I feel like I have been kicked by a mule!" Robert helped her up and back onto her horse. He walked over and picked up the snake and slung it over his shoulder. It drug the ground behind him. She said, "What are you doing?"

He said, "I am taking this snake to Cookie for dinner tonight!"

"You have got to be kidding!" Tonnie screeched.

He said, "No, I am not kidding." He turned and looked at her. "It taste like chicken you know!" She shivered. She would be definitely eating beef jerky tonight. She didn't care if

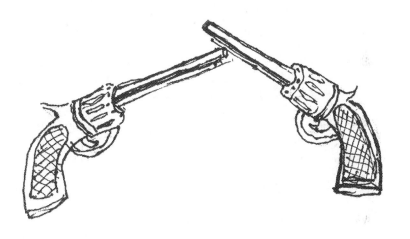

it did taste like chicken! She finished the day, but by the time they had stopped for the evening she was feeling the effects of the fall.

After a tuff and tumble day everyone began to bed down. She was so exhausted and sore she could barely move. Tonnie laid there thinking about Robert finding out who she really was, when she heard a noise. Someone was sneaking out of camp. But who she wondered.

She sat up on her bedroll, slipped into her boots, and followed. Claude Gibson was talking to a couple of men he met in a clump of trees. She heard him say. "I will get those papers, but you have to give me time. They are important to Mr. Devain, and I have to be careful." The other man said, "Well, you haven't got much time. We need them, and we need them now!" Claude said, "I will see what I can do."

Tonnie hobbled back to camp. When Claude came back Tonnie pulled her six-shooter on him. "Don't shoot Kid! It is me, Claude Gibson."

Robert was having a late night cup of coffee with Cookie. He peeked around the wagon when he heard what was happening. Claude looked over at him when Robert strolled over. "The kid pulled his gun on me boss. I couldn't sleep so I went for a walk. When I came back the kid decided he wanted to shoot me."

The boss told Tonnie, "Put the gun away! If you pull it on anyone else, I will take them away from you."

She said, "I'd like to see you try." Claude went on to bed. Tonnie looked at Robert. "How come you always stick your nose into my business? I was just getting it all straightened out."

"How? By killing someone?"

"No, but that isn't a bad ideal, you know." She turned to go back to her bedroll, and Robert gave her a swift kick in the seat of her pants. "Ouch!" After falling off her horse that day, his kick had hurt. "Cut it out Bobby. Some of the working people have to get some sleep!"

He said, "Don't call me Bobby! I don't want anymore of this gunplay. I mean it! You could be hurt." He seemed upset with her, but he just didn't understand. Besides she wasn't very pleased with him either.

Chapter 13

The next day was a scorcher in the hot sun. Tonnie

pulled her tired aching body into the saddle. Every bone and

muscle in her body throbbed. Robert rode up. He knew by

looking at her how she was feeling. He reached into his

saddlebag and got a bottle of whiskey. "Here, take a shot of

this. It will help with the pain." She took the bottle and had a

drink. She began to cough, spit, and sputter. It burnt all the

way down. He said, "Take another drink or two. It really will

help when it takes effect." She took two more drinks, and

handed the bottle back to him. After awhile she did start to

feel better. Robert was right.

They also ran into a dust storm. She wore her bandana over her face until it blew over. It was so miserable being so dirty. The river had been out of view most of the day, but where they chose to camp for the night it ran fairly close.

As soon as Robert noticed Tonnie missing, he went looking for her. She was sitting on a flat rock in the night breeze. Her wet hair, and clothes was evidence that she had taken a dip in the river to wash off some the dust. The bath had made her relaxed and feeling very good, considering how she had felt early in the day.

Robert walked toward her, and they were both startled. She pulled her gun in lighting fast fashion. She said, "Oh, Robert. Don't you know not to walk up on someone like that! I could have killed you!"

He was upset with her. Take those guns off! You have just pulled them on your last man!"

"No, I won't give them to you. They were Papa's, and I'm keeping them. I thought you were that Claude Gibson coming here to give me trouble. He burns me up the----she glanced over at Robert to see if he had noticed she had almost spilled obscenities. "Well, you need to watch out for him----that's all. He is up to no good." Of course she couldn't tell him why she felt that way.

He said, "You know Tonnie, sometimes you make me so mad I just want to turn you across my knee. Believe me, I have had to restrain myself on several occasions."

She slipped her arm out of his hold and went to camp before he could take her guns or do otherwise. Besides she didn't want their tempers to flare anymore than they already had.

Chapter 14

After Cookie had fed them, Robert rushed into the camp. He was furious. "Everyone listen up! Someone has taken some very important papers, and I want them back!" No one said anything. "If I don't find those papers there is going to be hell to pay!" He still didn't get any response.

He noticed Tonnie walk over to the black and begin to brush him down. When he went less noticed he made his way over to her. "Tonnie, do you know anything about my papers? I need them back!"

She looked at him. "Why would you think I know anything about them?" Of course she knew about them. She knew exactly who took them. She didn't want Robert to know that.

"I want my papers, and I want them now! They are really important. If this is your ideal of a joke it isn't funny!"

She looked at him. She couldn't believe he would suspect her of taking them. "I don't have them Robert. You will just have to trust me."

He shouted, "You better give me some answers Young lady!"

She shoved him. "Watch it Robert! Do you want to give away our secret? Then we would be in a real fine mess, wouldn't we?"

He turned and stomped off. He was so mad and upset. She hated to see him that way. He should know by now that when Tonnie had something to say, she said it, and nine times out of ten she was honest. He didn't have to worry about her, even though he did.

She would get his important papers back when the time was right. She just had to wait until she could figure out when that would be.

Chapter 15

The evening was intoxicating. Tonnie went out to the flat rock. She sat down, and decided to go wading. She took off her boots, and socks, and stepped into the cool water. It felt so good.

Robert walked up and spoiled the moment. "Come on out of there. I want to talk to you."

"What is the matter with you?" She asked.

He snapped back at her. "Don't ask so many questions, just do what you are told!"

She thought he was being bossier than a boss should be. She gave him a look, and climbed on the rock. She sat down to put her socks and boots on. She just barely had them back on when Robert was pulling her up to her feet.

"Robert, what is the matter with you?" He had a worried look on his face.

"Tonnie, I think you know more about my papers than you are telling me. If you knew how important they were to me you wouldn't be playing these games. You might say they are a matter of life and death."

She looked into his pleading eyes. She almost wished she did have something to tell him. She said, "I already told you. I don't know anything about your papers. You will just have to trust me on that. She started to walk off, and he grabbed her arm to prevent her from leaving.

"You know Tonnie, I am worried about you constantly."

"Worried about me? What on earth for?"

"A trail is no place for a woman. I told you that. Ever since I found out..... You are.... Well who you are, I can't take my eyes off of you even for a minute. It is just too dangerous. If the men were to find out about it.... He just shook his head thinking about it. "Well it just wouldn't be safe."

She said, "Robert, that pretty black hair of your is going to turn white if you don't stop worrying so much." She jerked her arm from his hold. "I told you I can take care of myself, and I don't need any help doing it." She was getting mad at him, and she stomped off to camp.

As she was fuming past some of the men began to taunt her. Being angry with Robert hadn't helped the situation. Was it because she was so young, or because she was supposedly a boy? What was it that made them constantly harass her?

Chapter 16

Pete said, "Hey kid, how about showing us how well you can shoot with those fancy irons you pack?" He started to laugh because he was only making fun of her. "You better be careful or you might shoot off your big toe." Everyone standing around him began to laugh.

By being mad at Robert her temper flared. She whipped out her six-shooter and shot a can on the ground five times as it pinged into the air with each shot. With the last of her bullets she shot a can out of Claude's hand. All laughter had stopped, as the men stood there not believing how well she could shoot. Her dad had taught her well.

This had been just a spur of the moment thing. She knew it was a mistake. But she had already made it. She put away her gun, and never stopped walking until she reached

camp. The little red headed freckle-faced boy that helped Cookie ran to meet her. "T-that was sure good shooting! You really showed them!"

She said, "Forget it! I shouldn't have lost my temper like that. It was a big mistake."

"No! No, it was great. I haven't ever seen anything like that. His eyes were as big as silver dollars. Cookie came up and started to scold him for not doing his chores. He ran off to do them before Cookie could say anything else.

Claude saw Robert walking to camp and was angry. "That kid could have taken my fingers off!"

Robert looked at him and said, "I saw the whole thing. I think he shoots well enough that he wouldn't have unless he was aiming at them."

It made Claude even more upset when he saw that Robert was going to take up for the kid. "Well, that just tears it. I quit! I have had all this abuse that I am going to take."

Robert reached into his shirt pocket and handed Claude his money. To say the least Robert was actually glad to be rid of him. He had the same feeling about him that Tonnie did.

He was nothing but a troublemaker. He didn't have a clue to how much of one he really was. Claude saddled his horse and rode away.

Chapter 17

After Robert had his dealings with Claude, he was so angry with Tonnie that he went looking for her. For once he was going to let her have it. When he found her at her favorite flat rock she was crying.

His heart softened. "Tonnie, what is the matter?"

"Oh, Robert. I was so angry at you that I made a fool out of myself. I should have just walked away from their sneers. I really made a mess of things. I just did it before I realized what I had done."

They were sitting on her rock, and he held her in his arms while she cried. It was almost as William used to hold her and let her cry after Aunt Effie had beaten her. She looked up at him. "Robert, I have something to tell you." She sat there speechless as if she didn't know where to begin.

He looked at her. "Well, what is it?"

"Well.... Here." She took off her hat. She handed him the papers he had been so upset over.

Now his temper flared. "So you have had them all along!" Before she could explain, he grabbed her and pulled her across his knee. Perhaps she hadn't handled the situation as well as she should have.

"Robert! You don't understand! Please!"

He began to whip her. She was furious at him. He was flying off the handle before finding out all the facts.

She was standing there looking up at him. She had tears in her dancing green eyes. "You had no right to do that!!!"

"What do you mean I had no right? I have been to my grave and back worrying about these papers. You knew that, and you have had them in you hat all this time. If that isn't right I don't know what is!"

"No, I didn't have them! I just got them. I took them out of Claude's thing's while you were talking to him. The night he snuck out of camp when I followed him, I heard him tell some

men that he would get them from you. I would have gotten it all straightened out, but you butted in that night. I guess it doesn't matter much now. You are rid of him."

He looked at her like he was having trouble believing her. At first he was speechless the he said, "Tonnie, I am so sorry! Please forgive me. It's just when I saw those papers I was so livid."

She looked at him. " It's all right Robert, but next time give me time to explain."

She was looking up at him deep into his wonderful blue eyes. He looked down into her dancing green eyes. Those terrific dancing green eyes of hers, and for the first time he let himself kiss her.

Chapter 18

Robert and Tonnie walked to the flat rock and they sat in the evening breeze. Robert broke the silence. "Tonnie, we will be in Richmond in a couple of days. I know you are plenty capable of taking care of yourself. I have seen it over and over on this drive, but I still worry about you. What if something goes wrong? For instance what if you don't find William?"

A fear shot through her. She hadn't even considered not finding him. Robert was scaring her. "You needn't worry about me. I will be all right. I will find William."

Robert said, "I know Tonnie, but what if it doesn't work out."

Fear began to sweep over her once again. She had never thought of that possibility.

It wasn't long until Tonnie made her way to camp. She was still trying to keep her identity a secret. The men were getting all spruced up to go to a town that was near by.

"Come on kid, go with us. We are going to get us a bottle of whiskey, a woman or maybe even two. We are going to have us one good time!" One of the men made a whooping sound at just the thought of it.

Robert stepped up and said, "The kid is staying here with me. I have to have help looking after the horses. It will keep him out of trouble. Speaking of trouble, if any of you gentlemen get into jail, then jail is where you will stay! Have a good time, but be careful, and use your head.

They all mounted their horses and rode off hooping, and hollering. Fun is what they had in mind.
Tonnie had gone over to cinch up her saddle. She was elected to watch the horses. She couldn't stop worrying about what Robert had said to her about William. What if she couldn't find him?

All of the sudden a shadow fell across her from the light of the campfire. She turned around suddenly to see someone standing there. "Who are you? What do you want?"
He began to laugh like he had been drinking all ready. "You don't fool me none Missy. I knowed you were a girl right from the start. A right pretty one at that." Pete stepped into the light. He began to try and take off her hat.

She pushed him away. "Get away from me! You've been drinking."

He began to try and steal a kiss. "I said, Stay away from me." He began to wrestle with her kind of rough to steal that kiss he was wanting. She reached for her gun. They were gone! Robert had taken them away from her for safekeeping. Oh, they were safe all right, but what about her?

She began to struggle with him, and try to talk him out of what he had in mind. Just as she began to think it was hopeless Robert grabbed him by his shirt and began to fight with him.

Robert and Pete had pretty big fistfight. Robert was so angry that Pete had tried force himself on Tonnie. When the

fight was over Robert threw Pete's pay at his feet on the ground beside him. "Get on your horse and get out of here! I don't ever want to see your face around here again. The next time I will kill you!"

Pete picked up his pay, stumbled to his horse and rode away. Robert rushed to Tonnie, who had been quite shaken by the ordeal.

"Tonnie, are you all right?" This encounter had left her trembling. "Tonnie, I won't let anyone ever hurt you again!"

All the sudden she was furious. She pushed Robert away. "This is all your fault."

"My fault? How do you figure?"

"If you hadn't taken my guns away he wouldn't even have a chance to get close enough to think such things." She turned to walk away.

Robert kicked her right in the seat of her pants. He was doing that much to often. "My fault? Come on fancy pants. I'll give you the guns back." Anyway he knew she would be able to take care of herself if she had her guns. She was right

and he knew it. He shouldn't have taken them away from her
in the first place.

Chapter 19

They reached Richmond two days later. Robert put the horses in the corral near the rail yard.

He made the deal with the buyer and was paid a fair price. Robert saw to it that the men were paid, and most of them went on their way. He had a very satisfied look on his face. Everything had worked out just as he planned.

He looked at Tonnie. "Come on Tonnie, Let's go get some of this inch thick dust off us."

She seemed in a rush. "Not now Robert! I want to go find William."

He grabbed her arm. "Hold on now. First we are going to get a bath, something to eat, rest, and then we will both go find William."

She was about to object, when Robert continued what he was saying. He was bent down looking into her eyes. His hat was almost touching her head. His head moved back and forth when he spoke. "The longer you stand here and argue with me, the longer it is going to take for you to find him."

He still had her arm, and was dragging her into the Hotel. He went to the desk with her in tow, and rang the little bell. The clerk turned around and said, "Yes."

Robert said, "We need two rooms. One for me, and one for the little lady here." With pen in hand he pointed at Tonnie.

The clerk frowned, and looked at Tonnie up and down. He sure didn't think she was a lady! Robert signed the register, and the manager handed him two keys. "We would like a hot bath also!"

Robert turned to Tonnie. "I have a few errands to run. You go ahead, get a bath and he handed her the keys. He smiled at her and walked out of the Hotel. Tonnie looked at the staring clerk and went upstairs. She supposed a hot bath would be nice at that. With soap and all. That would be so nice. She might want to soak for hours. It would be nice to

feel like a woman again.

Chapter 20

Once Robert had finished his errands on the way back to the Hotel he stopped at a Dress Shop. He told the woman about Tonnie. He needed a dress. He told her about what size she was, and to get everything that a woman would need.

He really didn't know what he was asking for, because the sales lady got everything she thought would be needed. He had about ten boxes when he left the store. He wouldn't have it any other way. He felt nothing was too good for Tonnie.

He managed to get the door open to her room, and dumped all the boxes on her bed. She was scrubbing in a tub of suds when he walked in on her. It was a good thing there were plenty of suds to cover her discreetly.

He was embarrassed anyway. "Oh, pardon me. I am looking for a sassy little trail hand. Would you happen to know which way she went?"

Tonnie laughed and threw her scrubbing sponge at him. He dodged it to keep from getting wet.

He picked up all her western wear and started out the door. "Hey! Bring back my clothes! What am I supposed to wear?"

He stopped at the door." That towel would be nice." He joked.

"Stop joking! I'm starving, and I can't get something to eat wearing only a towel."

"There are new things for you on the bed. I am going to go get cleaned up myself. He ran down the stairs, and handed her clothes to the Hotel manager. "Have these cleaned, and sent back to the little lady."

The clerk frowned and picked up her clothes like they were contaminated. Robert flipped a coin in the air for his trouble and the clerk caught it. Robert smiled and ran back upstairs to get that hot bath. He wouldn't mind to soak for a

while himself.

Chapter 21

He had shaved, taken a bath, dressed, and fell asleep on
the bed in the time it took her to get dressed. She had tapped
on his door, but he didn't hear her.

She tiptoed up to the bed and screamed as loud as she
could. He jumped straight into the air, and hit his head on
the headboard. He was rubbing the bump, still half asleep.
"Tonnie, what is the matter with you?"

"Nothing is the matter with me. I am ready to go get
something to eat. She looked so stunning in the dress he
bought her. He gave her an evil eye. He picked her up, and
swung her petite body around and around.

"Tonnie, you are as pretty as an angel, but to
mischievous to be one I am afraid."

They went downstairs to the dining room to get something to eat. Tonnie stuffed herself. Beans were practically all they had seen since the day they left for Richmond.

She stood up, and made the announcement that she was ready to go. "Ready to go where?" Robert inquired.

"To find my brother, William. What do you think?"

Robert said, "First I want you to rest. Then I will rent us a buggy, and we will see if we can find him."

She stomped her foot in disagreement. "I don't want to rest! I want to find William. If you don't want to go, then I will go by myself."

"If you will be a good girl, and rest first, I will take you to find William." He was pushing her along, as if he thought she would listen to him.

"I said I don't want to rest!"

He said, "Do you remember how on the trail I lost my head and whipped you? You are going to rest first!" Her dancing green eyes were proof that she was angry. He picked her up over his shoulder and carried her upstairs. He put her down, and pushed her into her room, and shut the door.

She was screaming at him. "You are not my boss anymore! You can't make me stay in here."

He pulled him a chair out of his room, and sat in the hallway. After a while he leaned back against the wall, and pulled his hat down for a short nap. He had come to know Tonnie so well. She would probably try to sneak away. He was having great fun teasing with her.

He just got comfortable when the door began to slowly squeak. She was in fact trying to sneak out.

"Where do you think you are going?"

He startled her. "Oh! Robert."

He sat all four legs of the chair on the floor. Tonnie opened her door and ran back inside her room. She slammed the door in disgust and screamed.

Chapter 22

About an hour later Tonnie came out of her room.
Robert had fallen asleep in the chair that was leaning against
the wall. Tonnie said, "Robert, wake up! I want to go find
William."

He felt like he had taunted her enough so he stood up
and stretched. Sitting in the chair to sleep had left him stiff.

"It serves you right." Tonnie said. He ignored her, and
put the chair back in his room. They went to the stable to
rent a buggy. Robert was talking to the man at the stable and
found out that a young man had bought a farm not to long ago
about two miles from town. Tonnie was sure it had to be
William.

Robert drove the buggy about where the man had told
him. Soon they came upon a small farm. A man and a small

boy were working in the field. Tonnie looked at Robert. "It must not be William. These people have children."

Chickens were running about, and there was a cow, and calf in the corral.

All of the sudden Tonnie screamed, "It is William!" She was trying to get out of the buggy before Robert could bring it to a stop. "William! William!"

The man in the field was trying to shade his eyes to see who was calling his name. Tonnie was running toward them. "Tonnie? Tonnie is that you?" She already had her arms around him.

He was so excited to see her, and couldn't believe she was really here. The small boy said, "Who is this lady, Pa?" Tonnie was shocked. This small boy had called her brother Pa.

A small frail woman was walking toward them from the house. She was wiping her hands on her apron. William said, "Look honey! This is my sister, Tonnie. I just can't believe you are here. Tonnie, this is my wife Sally, and this is her son Alan." He rustled Alan's hair in a loving gesture. "Huh, as

you can see we are going to have another one soon." He pointed at Sally, who was smiling, and blushing.

Tonnie had been speechless. William having a family had thrown her completely off guard.

Robert stepped out of the buggy. Tonnie said, "Oh, this is Robert Devain. He is the man that helped me come here to find you. I sort of hid as a trail hand to help him bring a string of horses to Richmond. It worked out well until he discovered who I was. They were all walking toward the house as she was telling William all about it.

Chapter 23

Sally invited everyone into the house for pie, and coffee. At first it was a little uncomfortable, but Robert began to tell the stories of how Tonnie had come about getting to Richmond.

He told William how she had hired on the trail ride as a boy, and how he didn't catch on until half way through the ride. "I should have figured it out by her dancing green eyes." They all began to laugh.

Robert and William got along well, and visited for hours. Of course Robert had lots of stories to tell about Tonnie. Alan was having great fun listening to all the stories. He especially liked the story about the rattlesnake.

Robert was saying, "I was going to send her back, but she informed me how important it was that she found you. She wouldn't have stayed even if I sent her back. Whether or not you know it, she is headstrong. I certainly have had my hands full. He smiled. It has been a pleasure."

Robert finally said, "It is getting late. I need to get back to the stable with the buggy."

Tonnie stood up and said, "Yes, we really must be getting back to town."

William said, "Tonnie, I thought maybe you would stay with us."

She said, "Oh, no I have a room in town. Thank you so much for the pie and coffee Sally." She gave her a hug, and walked to the door with Robert.

She turned and hugged William. "It was so good to see you again, brother." She smiled trying to hide her disappointment. "I was so glad to hear from you and to know that you were alright."

She went to the buggy, and Robert helped her step into it. They waved good-bye and rode away. Robert could tell that Tonnie was upset. She was to quiet. So quiet it was frightening. Robert had never known her to be like that.

He finally got the courage to talk to her. "Tonnie, are you all right?"

She didn't say anything, and she didn't cry until he put his arm around her. "Oh, Robert. What am I going to do now? William doesn't need me. He has Sally and Alan. You were right! Things just haven't worked out like I planned. Now I don't know what I am going to do." She was really sobbing. "I just can't go back to Aunt Effie and have her make me marry that sissy man, Benton."

Robert held her closer as the buggy trudged along the road. "Tonnie, I don't like to see you this way. I tried to tell you this might happen."

"I know! I just didn't listen." She was really crying. "I'm sorry, Robert. I feel so helpless, so alone. I don't know what to do."

At that point he stopped the buggy. He looked at her. "Tonnie, you are far from being alone. I am here with you. Can't you see me right here with you?"

She smiled a little smile. "Yes, but you have your own life. You certainly don't want me hanging around, messing it up."

He was still looking down at her. "Haven't I taken good care of you so far?"

"Yes, but..."

"Have I complained about you being around so far?"

"No, but..."

"Tonnie, in case you don't know it I am hopelessly in love with you. I love everything about you. I love your dancing green eyes when you are excited or angry. I even love the way you are so sassy."

She looked at him. He said, "What I am trying to say is that I want you to marry me. I want to have you around in my life forever. I want to take care of you always."

"Oh, Robert." They kissed each other tenderly. He held her close, and had the team start up again. The buggy went on its way to town. She was smiling now. Her tears were gone.

Not long after they were married there was a knock on the door. When Tonnie opened the door there stood Aunt Effie's servant, Rosa. Tonnie was so glad to see her. Rosa told her that their Aunt Effie had passed on.

She had seen to it that she was buried in the cemetery with all the other family.

Aunt Effie had given Rosa the fare to find Tonnie and William and let them know that she had left them everything she owned. Rosa said, "That includes me. I am here to take care of you and your mister, just like I took care of Miss Effie. She said I was to make sure I took good care of you. You see she did love you even though she was cruel. She always regretted how she done you. She hated it when you slipped off. That is why she wanted you kids to have everything."

Tonnie grabbed Rosa and hugged her. "Oh Rosa! I am so glad you are here. I know you will love it here with us. You are part of our family." Rosa would have the job for as long as she wanted it. Tonnie hoped she would want it forever. Tonnie's life was perfect now. She was close to Willliam and his family and she had met the love of her life. Just days ago they hadn't even known each other..... And to think it all started on a small bridge in Aunt Effie's hometown. She was truly grateful to Aunt Effie for that.